Frosty the Snowman

This book belongs to:

....

Frosty the Snowman

During the night, the first big snow of the winter had fallen. The next morning was bright and sunny. The children came out of their houses and began to roll balls of snow. They had two large snowballs in no time.

After placing one large snowball on top of the other, the children rolled a third snowball that was just the right size for a head. Tommy brought pieces of coal for the eyes and a button for the nose. "Here's a straw broom for him to carry," said Karen.

"These old rubber boots will be great for the snowman," said Jimmy.

"He can wear my old mittens and scarf," giggled Lindsay.

"All he needs now is a hat," the children agreed. Karen found an old ball cap, but it just wouldn't stay on the snowman's head.

Tommy tried an old, tattered hat that his dad wore fishing, but that wasn't right either.

The wind began to whistle and blow. As if by magic, a shiny, black top hat came blowing across the snow-covered yard and came to rest at the children's feet. Lindsay reached down, picked up the hat, and placed it on the snowman's head.

All at once, the snowman began to speak! "Hi, boys and girls! I'm Frosty the Snowman," he said.

That is how the adventures of Frosty the Snowman began.

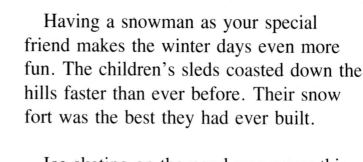

Having a snowman as your special friend makes the winter days even more fun. The children's sleds coasted down the hills faster than ever before. Their snow fort was the best they had ever built.

Ice skating on the pond was never this much fun before. Amazingly, the children didn't get cold and shivery with Frosty nearby. They weren't sure if it was the warmth of Frosty's heart or the magic of his smile. It didn't matter why . . . they were having a wonderful time.

Each day, Frosty surprised the children with an exciting, new adventure. "I've never seen a store," Frosty told the children one day. "I'd like to go shopping," he grinned. "What a great idea!" exclaimed Lindsay. "I know where there is a great toy store," added Tommy. Singing merrily, they started towards town.

Frosty and the children loved to look into the brightly decorated store windows. Their eyes were wide with excitement! The children led Frosty all around the streets of town in the warm, winter sunshine.

Frosty and the children were on a busy street corner where a policeman was directing traffic. Suddenly, a warm gust of wind blew Frosty's hat into the street!

The policeman whistled the children to a stop. They were unable to follow Frosty as he chased his hat down the street.

As soon as the traffic light turned green, the children raced down the street to find Frosty. His shiny, black top hat was still rolling through the melted snow, but there was no Frosty!

"Frosty the Snowman is gone! Do you know where he is?" the children asked the policeman.

"When the winter sun is warm and bright, all snowmen disappear. But Frosty will be back again with a cold and snowy day," answered the policeman.

And you know . . . the policeman is right! Frosty will be back again someday soon!